A LIFT-THE-FLAP STORY

What Is Hanukkah?

Harriet Ziefert • Pictures by Rick Brown

■ HarperFestival

A Division of HarperCollins*Publishers*

"Come and help me polish the menorah," said Josh's mother. "Tomorrow is the first night of Hanukkah."

"What is Hanukkah?" asked Josh.

"Hanukkah is a Jewish holiday,
which comes in early winter.
On Hanukkah, Jews remember miracles
that happened a long, long time ago."

"The first miracle happened when Judah Maccabee and a small band of Jews defeated the army of King Antiochus, a mean and wicked man who wanted the Jews to stop worshiping one God."

Josh's father said, "The second miracle happened when Judah and the Maccabees were rebuilding the Temple that King Antiochus had destroyed. The Maccabees found a menorah in the Temple with enough oil to keep the lamp lit for only one day. But, miracle of miracles, the oil burned for a full eight days."

Then Josh's mother said, "On the first night of Hanukkah, we all gather around the menorah. Daddy says a blessing and lights the first candle. On the second night, we will light two candles. Then three, then four...until, by the eighth night, all eight candles will be lit."

"What's a dreidel?" asked Josh.

"On Hanukkah," said Josh's grandma, "we eat potato *latkes*."

"On Hanukkah, we exchange presents."

"Then we sing:
   I have a little dreidel. I made it out of clay.
   And when it's dry and ready, then dreidel I shall play."

Happy Hanukkah!